# God Gave Us Thankful Hearts

by Lisa Tawn Bergren    art by David Hohn

WATERBROOK

*To Ava and Wrenna—I'm so thankful for you!*
*Love, Aunt Lisa*

*For Joon, my very own Little Pup.*

GOD GAVE US THANKFUL HEARTS

Hardcover ISBN 978-1-60142-874-5
eBook ISBN 978-1-60142-875-2

Text copyright © 2016 by Lisa Tawn Bergren

Illustrations copyright © 2016 by David Hohn

Cover design by Mark D. Ford; cover illustration by David Hohn

Published in the United States by WaterBrook, an imprint of the Crown Publishing Group, a division of Penguin Random House LLC, New York.

WATERBROOK® and its deer colophon are registered trademarks of Penguin Random House LLC.

Library of Congress Cataloging-in-Publication Data
Names: Bergren, Lisa Tawn. | Hohn, David, 1974– illustrator.
Title: God gave us thankful hearts / Lisa Tawn Bergren ; illustrated by David Hohn.
Description: First edition. | Colorado Springs, Colorado : WaterBrook Press, 2016.
Identifiers: LCCN 2016011538 (print) | LCCN 2016029573 (ebook) | ISBN 9781601428745 (hardback) | ISBN 9781601428752 (electronic)
Subjects: | CYAC: Gratitude—Fiction. | Autumn—Fiction. | Seasons—Fiction. | Christian life—Fiction. | Wolves—Fiction. | BISAC: JUVENILE FICTION / Religious / Christian / Family. | JUVENILE FICTION / Family / General (see also headings under Social Issues). | JUVENILE FICTION / Animals / General.
Classification: LCC PZ7.B452233 Goo 2016 (print) | LCC PZ7.B452233 (ebook) | DDC [E]—dc23
LC record available at https://lccn.loc.gov/2016011538

Printed in the United States of America
2016—First Edition

10 9 8 7 6 5 4 3 2 1

SPECIAL SALES
Most WaterBrook books are available at special quantity discounts when purchased in bulk by corporations, organizations, and special-interest groups. Custom imprinting or excerpting can also be done to fit special needs. For information, please e-mail specialmarketscms@penguinrandomhouse.com or call 1-800-603-7051.

"Well, there you are,
Little Pup," Mama said.
"Why are you looking
so glum?"

"I dunno," he mumbled.
"I'm just sad."

"How can you be sad on
such a beautiful day?"

"Because the leaves are changing colors and
soon it will be winter. I like spring, summer, and fall when
I can play with all my friends! Hibernatin' season is boring."

"You'll still have some friends about come winter. And there's
a reason for us to be thankful in *every* season, Little Pup."

"We need winter to let the land—and some of your friends—have a rest. Otherwise, we wouldn't get spring!"

"But everyone is going to be hibernatin'!" he grumbled. "The chipmunks and bears, the badgers and bats. Even the raccoons, beavers, and squirrels won't come out much."

"What about the skunks or bees? You won't see much of *them* either," Mama said.

Little Pup smiled. "I guess I could be thankful about *that*."

"We can be thankful for how God paints our forest every autumn," Mama said.

"Yeah, but I'm not thankful for poison ivy," Little Pup said, remembering the time he rolled in a patch by accident. "It makes you sooo itchy!"

"True. But you can be thankful you know how to avoid it now, right?"

"I guess…"

"Oh, and I'm not thankful when my pack buddies get too rammunktious with me," Little Pup said.

"Rambunctious, you mean?"

"Yeah, that."

Mama giggled. "But you can be thankful you have friends who will be around all winter, right? They will keep you from being lonely."

"Maybe…"

"The trick to having a thankful heart," Mama said,
"is thinking about the things that make us happy,
rather than the things that don't."

"Hmm. Like what?"

"Well, that's easy. I'm thankful
for *you,*" she said,
squeezing him tight.
"Being your mama has made
me one of the happiest
mamas in the
whole wide world."

"And you, Little Pup? What makes you thankful?"

"Well, you and Papa, o' course," he said.

"And I'm thankful for fishing!"

"I like fishing too," Papa said. "But God gave us thankful hearts so we could praise him even when we don't catch fish."

"*What?* That's crazy talk!" Little Pup said.

"It's not," Papa said, with a smile.
"We can be thankful for this last bit of autumn
and time together beside this beautiful river.
*Even* if we don't catch fish."

"I'm thankful we go to the harvest festival
every year!" Little Pup said.
"But I didn't like it when we got
lost in the corn maze."

"Me either," Mama said. "But we found our way through, right? We can be thankful for how God shows us the way, even when it seems a little scary."

"Yeah. And that we're not alone in those times," Little Pup said.

"Yes! Now you're getting the hang of having a thankful heart."

"My heart is thankful for apples!"
Little Pup said.

"Mmm," Mama said. "And hot apple pie."

"Oooh, yes. And caramel apples," Papa said.
"Or baked apples with ice cream!"

"I'm thankful for the freedom to wander and explore," Mama said. "And for this pretty country we live in."

"Me too," Little Pup said.

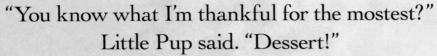

"You know what I'm thankful for the mostest?"
Little Pup said. "Dessert!"

"And for dinner before it," Mama said, lifting a brow.
"Something healthy in our bellies before all this sugar."

"I'm thankful for our cozy warm home," Papa said.
"Especially as winter draws near."

Little Pup had to admit he was really sleepy as he yawned and climbed the stairs toward bed. He felt so thankful he was with his mama and papa inside and not out in the damp forest or cold wet snow.

"I'm glad I don't feel sad anymore," Little Pup said. "I'm glad God gave me a thankful heart."

"Us too, Little Pup," Mama said.
"We all have so much to be thankful for."

Little Pup drifted off to sleep with a smile on his face,
thanking God for his friends and family…and for fishing…
and for corn mazes…and for apples…

And for changing seasons.

*Even*…for the end of fall.